About the Author

My background includes a Bachelor of Arts in Child Development from Cal Poly Humboldt in Northern California. My career includes working in daycare preschool and K through eighth grade schools. My favorite job was working in the special-ed class for seventh and eighth grade students. I hope you enjoy the book.

> # Pieces

Maya Rain

Pieces

Olympia Publishers
London

www.olympiapublishers.com
OLYMPIA PAPERBACK EDITION

Copyright © Maya Rain 2023

The right of Maya Rain to be identified as author of
this work has been asserted in accordance with sections 77 and 78 of
the Copyright, Designs and Patents Act 1988.

All Rights Reserved

No reproduction, copy or transmission of this publication
may be made without written permission.
No paragraph of this publication may be reproduced,
copied or transmitted save with the written permission of the publisher,
or in accordance with the provisions
of the Copyright Act 1956 (as amended).

Any person who commits any unauthorised act in relation to
this publication may be liable to criminal
prosecution and civil claims for damage.

A CIP catalogue record for this title is
available from the British Library.

ISBN: 978-1-80439-570-7

This is a work of fiction.
Names, characters, places and incidents originate from the writer's
imagination. Any resemblance to actual persons, living or dead, is
purely coincidental.

First Published in 2023

Olympia Publishers
Tallis House
2 Tallis Street
London
EC4Y 0AB

Printed in Great Britain

Dedication

To my best friends Sharon and Neal Sligh.

Acknowledgements

To Jennifer Allen for her technological assistance. To Carrie Brown for her encouragement.

Pieces

My world
My worlds
Too many worlds
Pieces
Of a puzzle
That don't fit
Together
Maybe,
I can be
The piece
That fits
In between
Maybe,
I can be
A bridge
And bring
Understanding

Maya Rain

How Do You Rate?

The bell rang. The ring grew louder and louder almost in my ear. Karen was running around from dorm to dorm ringing that stupid bell. "All right, already," Lisa shouted at her. "We're up."

I crunched down in my covers. I felt so warm and safe inside my covers, it was like floating inside a warm cloud. I sure hated to wake up, but I could hear the girls opening and shutting their lockers so I very slowly sat up in bed with my covers wrapped completely around me. I blinked a few times and saw that everyone in my dorm, except me, was up and in the process of getting dressed. I stuck my feet out from under my covers and started to stand up. The floor was cold and my feet began to immediately throb with pain.

Then I remembered that this day I was going to County Hospital to have my feet operated on. Immediately I felt excited and dressed in a hurry. I pulled three pairs of soft socks over my feet... I found that this made it easier to walk. Still, when I walked, I felt like I was walking on hot straight pins. I had counted, altogether, I had nine purple sores on the bottom of my feet which my PO (Probation Officer) said were plantar warts. I'd complained to the staff where I lived but they just gave me aspirin. Finally, when my PO came to see me, I showed her my feet. I was beginning to limp and my friends would tease me and call me Grandma Kinzer.

My PO seemed worried. "I'll arrange for transportation to take you, though the earliest will probably be next week," she told me.

I grabbed my clothes from the locker next to my bed, then I dressed myself sitting on my bed so I wouldn't have to stand more than necessary. Then while I was scooting around trying to make my bed the breakfast bell rang. I hobbled through the gigantic kitchen. I took a beige plate off the counter. "All right," I thought, "my favourite, French toast." The syrup was almost gone so I hit the bottom of the syrup bottle a few times.

I went to the dining room which was probably the largest room in the detention centre. There were close to two hundred girls, eating and talking, at rows of long narrow tables. The staff all sat together at the table closest to the kitchen. I was anxious to find Sue, my "tight", which means good friend. I tried not to look anxious, though, and I walked slowly holding my plate.

"Hey, Kinzer, over here." I was relieved to see Sue wave. I sat down and while I was eating, I noticed that everyone at the table was watching me.

"Man, how do you rate?" Jessee asked between bites of French toast.

I shrugged, but I was excited, too. It was worth one hundred plantar warts, to me, just to get out of there for one day.

I was twelve and I had been locked up in the detention centre for six months. Mrs Whitehead stood up and rang a loud tin bell. The dining room was quiet, instantly. "Kinzer, where's Kinzer?" she bellowed. I stood up quickly and hobbled over to the staff table. "Transportation here for you. Hurry up," she said.

I followed Mrs Whitehead to the front reception office. She took a key for her chain and unlocked the door that opened up into the office. It felt strange to me to go in that office. The last time I'd been in that office was six months before when my PO brought me there straight from Juvenile Hall. Mrs Whitehead searched me methodically as they did when I came in form the hall.

I wondered what she thought I could get between the dining hall and the office.

I followed the transportation lady out the front door. Then I realized I was holding my breath. I let my breath come out slowly and felt the way a person must feel when they've been under the water too long and they finally come up for air.

Everything looked so different. The trees, the sky, they day, it all seemed to be saying to me, "Here we are waiting for you to live in." The day seemed to me like a brand-new toy just after it was unwrapped on Christmas. I got in the white car that had a circle on the side that said 'US Government'.

"I have to make a stop at Mac before I take you to County," she told me crisply. "You'll have to wait until they're ready for you in the waiting room at court with some kids from Mac." I shrugged. Mac was short for Maclaren Hall and the kids form Mac went to the same court the kids from Juvenile Hall went to. The County Hospital was right next to it.

The little girl from Mac was, maybe, six or seven with big dark eyes and curly hair. She stared out the car window at the LA freeway the same as I did. I felt the car moving so fast by everything and I thought how strange it was that the car could move so fast and cover in only five minutes a space that a person like me could spend six months in.

The transportation lady parked in front of the juvenile court building in East LA We went inside. The hall was long with narrow benches lined against the wall. The smell of the place was antiseptic like a hospital. I saw police walking and a child crying.

We went into the waiting room. There was a lady sitting at the desk who looked sleepy and there were a few painted white benches to sit on. There were also a few wooden cribs lining the wall. "What do we have here?" the lady at the desk asked.

"One from Mac and one in custody." She nodded towards me. "She's scheduled for surgery at County," the transportation lady said in an official sounding voice.

I sat down next to one of the wooden cribs. I looked in the crib and saw a baby about six months old waving her arm in the air. She was making cooing noises. I noticed how cute the baby was. She had big brown eyes and black hair. Then I saw that her other arm and one leg were in casts.

Two tall policemen came into the room. They leaned over the crib and smiled and tickled the baby. The baby laughed and the police talked baby talk back to her.

Watching, I felt very sad and lonely. I felt sad for the baby and for myself I felt lonely. I suddenly wished my PO wasn't on vacation. My lost feeling came over me which I think is how Luke Skywalker must have felt when he fell into outer-space. It was like falling with nothing solid to grab on to.

The phone rang. The woman at the desk answered it and looked at me. "That was County," she told the police. "She's going to outpatient. I need someone to take her over and bring her back."

"I'll take her over," said one of the cops who had been playing with the baby. He motioned me to follow him. I limped after him.

"What's wrong with your feet?" he asked.

"Oh," I answered, "I have plantar warts."

"Gee," he said sympathetically, "that must really hurt."
"Yeah," I answered him. "It does kind of hurt…"

Solitary

No one
But one
Who has
No one
At all
Knows how it feels
To cry
On a wall
Four walls in your face
A lock on the door
A sink over there
A hard cement floor
It wouldn't be bad
If someone were there
But no one is there
No one at all

Spunky

Maya smiled to herself as she looked at the collage she had just made. On one side were pictures of cute cuddly babies while the other side had pictures of starving babies and children.

"That's not what I had in mind." Her teacher frowned.

Maya turned away and shrugged. "I don't care," she thought, "this collage says what I want it to say. Some babies are loved and some aren't."

The bell rang, ending Maya's day at LaPuente High School. Maya walked home slowly, holding onto her collage. A brief fleeting memory stopped her from walking. She saw herself at seven or eight running home from school, eager to show her work to her mother. Maya felt sad and lonely for her mother. Then she told herself, "Don't be a baby, you're almost fifteen. You don't need a mother any more. Besides, you have spunky."

Maya had become a ward of the state at age twelve and lived in a foster home.

She had found Spunky, her puppy, at the Golden Gate Horse Stables. She went there as often as she could to admire the horses.

One day she spotted a cardboard box full of puppies. She was playing with the puppies when an old man appeared.

"What kind of puppies are these?" Maya asked.

"Mutts Heinz fifty-seven," the old man spat.

"What are you going to do with them?"

"Drown them," the old man said. "They're worthless."

"Can I take one?"

"I don't care."

Maya had taken the puppy she held and named him Spunky.

She stopped walking and gazed at her collage. Her foster parents, Bert and Alice, had been friendly at first. Bert had praised her for being a hard worker while she cleaned the house. Alice liked the fact that she did the dishes and cleaned the kitchen. Then Bert had been too friendly. He pressed hard against her while she was washing the dishes.

"Don't," Maya said angrily.

Bert's beefy red face glistened with sweat. "You think you're too good for me?" he hissed at her.

Since then, things had gone very wrong. Maya blinked at her collage, remembering the night before. She had let Spunky into the kitchen to feed him. Alice was cooking at the stove and kicked Spunky hard as he walked by. Spunky had flown across the kitchen floor squealing.

"You bitch," Maya yelled hot with rage. "You kick my puppy again and I'll kick you."

Maya picked Spunky up and took him outside the kitchen door, to the backyard. He was shaking and whimpering. She sat and soothed Spunky while she talked to him.

"I'm sorry, Spunky," she whispered, "Alice is an old witch. They'll be kicking me out of here, for sure, now that I've gone and called Alice a bitch."

She stroked Spunky while she continued talking. "I'll have to find some way to take you with me. I'm not supposed to have a puppy in a foster home. Don't worry. I'll think of something," Maya said worriedly.

She laid down in a large cardboard box she had found for him. Then she covered him with a blanket.

"Goodnight," she whispered.

Startled, Maya glanced at her collage. Suddenly, Maya was frightened. "What if they hurt Spunky, today, while I'm at school?" she thought.

Maya ran the rest of the way home still holding tight to her collage. She was relieved to find Spunky playing in the backyard. Spunky ran to her. He jumped up and licked her. Maya sat and held Spunky gently. Her foster sister, Lisa, came outside and told her that her social worker was coming to pick her up today. Maya sat still, very worried. She thought hard about what she could do. Then she went to the bathroom where she searched the medicine chest, frantically. Relieved, she spotted some Sominex. She shook two Sominex tablets into her hand. Then she mixed her dog's food with the crushed Sominex. She called for Spunky to come and eat. Maya set the bowl of food in front of Spunky. Then she went into the bedroom she shared with two other girls and packed her few belongings into a cardboard box. Next, praying that her idea worked, Maya tried to relax. Then she heard tiny yelping noises coming from the backseat. Mrs Catts pulled over onto the shoulder of the road.

"Maya, do you have a dog in here?" she asked.

"Yes."

Maya leaned over to the backseat and pulled Spunky out of the box. She held him while Spunky wiggled and licked her.

"Oh," exclaimed Mrs Catts, "he's so cute. What's his name?"

"Spunky."

"Look, Maya they won't let you keep him at the home but I'll take care of him until I can find a good home for him. So don't worry."

Maya held Spunky gently as they drove onto the Los Angelos freeway. She wasn't worried any more.

Stay strong

What do I do
When all is wrong?
How do I stay
Strong?

Where do I turn
When life is cruel
To keep from doing
What makes
One a fool?

What's Normal?

She stood hesitantly waiting for the house charge to recognize her. The charge was in deep conversation with Lynn, one of Maya's roommates. From what Maya could make out, Lynn was having a 'number' (one of Lynn's ways of getting attention). Ruth, the house mother, looked up abruptly, giving Maya an annoyed look.

"I just thought I'd tell you; I'm not going to work tomorrow because my social worker's picking me up at eight thirty," Maya said in one long breath. It was a standard house rule that you be up and out by eight.

"Where are you going?" Ruth asked.

"I'm leaving. I'm going to a foster home and back to school," Maya stated defiantly.

"Well, I hope you know what you're doing," Ruth said flippantly.

"I know what I'm doing," Maya replied firmly.

"OK, it's up to you," Ruth stated with a note of finality.

Getting ready for bed, Maya stepped over the two girls on the floor in sleeping bags. She dug around in the crowded closet and managed to get her few things together in a sack ready to go.

Lying in bed staring into the darkness, Maya's thoughts raced. She wasn't really sorry to go, although there were a few girls she would miss. If Joe the head person would've let her go to school, maybe she would've stayed. Maya had gone to work on the bus watching other kids laugh and talk on their way to school. She'd envied them intensely. She'd rebelled inside against her life. She felt as though she was being forced into a corner, being forced into living an adult life when she wasn't ready, yet.

That morning, instead of getting off the bus at her stop, she had just stayed on the bus. Finding her way to the welfare office, she told the social worker, "I want to go to school, but they won't let me." She hadn't told the social worker that she didn't want to grow up yet. That she wanted to go to football games, dances, and everything else that a "normal" teenager does.

Maya was being honest when she said she wanted to go to school. For her, school was the only way out — the only way to a better life.

Morning came with Sue her friend squeezing her hand tightly.

"Goodbye," Sue whispered softly. "Good luck."

Later, Maya sat at the kitchen table watching the clock nervously.

"Why are you leaving?" Tom asked her. He startled her.

She'd been so lost in her thoughts she hadn't noticed him.

"I want a normal life," Maya answered him.

Tom looked at her contemptuously.

"Normal, what's normal?" he asked sarcastically...

Maya looked at him without answering.

Normal is a home, love, school and friends. Normal is something I want very badly, she thought.

Ruth sauntered into the kitchen. "Your social worker's here," she announced. As Maya started to grab her things, Ruth added, "Come back some time and visit."

"Sure," Maya answered, knowing she wouldn't.

For a minute Maya was scared. Then is passed and was replaced with hope.

"Good morning," said the well-dressed social worker as Maya walked toward her.

"Good morning," Maya replied.

Homeless Child

Homeless child, running wild
The streets, reach out to claim you.
Will they?
Homeless child, shivering in the dark
Wondering if it's safe
Again
To sleep in the park?

Homeless child running for your life
Behind you
Stalking

A man with a knife.
Homeless child, running from the law
While tearing hunger pains
Begin to gnaw

Homeless child, in a tiny little cell
With a thousand other children
An institution
Made in hell

Homeless child, free again
To roam the streets once more
And you begin to wonder

What you're living for.

Homeless child, warm tears in the night
You've nowhere to go
You shiver with cold
You shiver with fright.

Homeless child, the welfare's
Got you now
They put you in a home
Where the people
Somehow
Aren't real.

So, you split
The streets
Again
You learn to lie, to fight, to steal
But most important
You learn to feel
Life

Homeless child, you make your
First score
Somehow you know
You're not a child any more
You watch a junkie fix
While a pusher stands there
Smelling bad
You been had.

Homeless child, grown up now
Living in a different world
Trying hard to understand
Different people
Different rules
Holding tight to God's hand

Homeless child, crying inside
"Cause" people are so blind
To all
The
Homeless children
You left
Behind
Maya

Sunkist

I met Deena, my sister, when I was a freshman at Long Beach City College. She sat down across the table from me in the school's cafeteria. A mutual friend introduced us. I looked at her. She was sleepy and rubbed her eyes. Her red hair was tousled and she smiled at me in an open, friendly way. When I got to know her better, I nicknamed her Sunkist because she reminded me of an orange, wholesome and healthy. The turning point in our friendship came, at least to me, the first year I knew her, we ran around in bear costumes at my school. We were both having a great deal of fun and the eyes in my costumes were too high up and I couldn't see so I spent my time holding on to Deena and stumbling around. When I pulled off the head of my costume, Deena was laughing at me and she gave me a hug, threw her arms around me and said "I love you." Then happiness went through me and I looked at her, and I loved her back.

    I remember us building a fire on the beach at night, singing, roasting hotdogs and marshmallows. We became roommates and on Thanksgiving we decided to go camping. This was quite an adventure. Before we even left, someone in Deena's family had to call the police about a disturbance. We went by to make sure everything was all right. Deena drove and Suzanne and I looked out the window, talked, sang and sometimes argued with each other.

    We stopped in San Luis Obispo for coffee at Howard Johnson's and Deena locked her keys in the car. It was pouring rain, late at night and in the middle of nowhere by the freeway, so Deena called the automobile club. After we started again, we drove straight through the night and arrived in San Jose at about four thirty a.m. Deena wanted to stop and say hi to some of her friends. It was too early to call her friends so we drove to a skate park to sleep until about six thirty. I set the alarm and we all laid down in our sleeping bags to sleep but none of us could sleep. We decided to have breakfast in a restaurant to kill time. Deena put the alarm clock in her purse and we forgot about it. While we were ordering breakfast, the alarm clock in the handbag went off; it was very loud and shrill. At first, we were embarrassed because the waitress gave us a strange look. Deena dug frantically in her handbag to stop the alarm. Then we all laughed. Later that day we got lost and couldn't find the campground we were looking for so we went to a local CHP to ask for directions. The police offered to let us camp in their parking lot but none of us wanted to do that. We hadn't come all the way from LA to sleep in a parking lot. Finally, late that night we pulled into a beautiful camp ground in San Mateo. We all crawled into our sleeping bags, exhausted. It started to rain but I was too tired to care. Suzanne groaned and Deena mumbled.

I lived with Deena and her family for a while. There are many qualities about Deena that I respect and admire. One is that she accepts people as people and even if she didn't like what you were doing there was always still that acceptance and caring underneath the disagreements. I shared a room with Deena, Judy, Donna and sometimes the dog. Deena loved that dog but I didn't. She liked to cuddle up to him at night and since I shared the bed with her, I was not too happy about this. The dog would make a lot of licking noises and try to cuddle up to me which I didn't like at all. So, I made Deena keep the dog on her side. She did. After she fell asleep, the dog would move over to my side and try to lick me so I'd pick him up and put him outside. We had a few arguments about this but we never really reached an agreement.

Sometimes I felt like Deena was too nice to people. Gale, a friend we knew, would come over and turn the channel on the TV even if I was already watching something. I got in a few arguments with him about this. What would really bug me is that he would order Deena around. He would plop down on the couch and say, "Deena, get me a glass of water." So, one day I said, "Gale, get it yourself, she's not your slave." Deena was also more of a diplomat than I. One day all of us wanted to go skating so I was sitting in Deena's car with two friends and Deena was out talking because there was a disagreement as to which skating rink to go to. I didn't care just as long as we went. Finally, after about ten minutes, I got tired of waiting so I just started Deena's car and drove her car very slowly down the street. This kind of scared Deena because I didn't have my driver's licence yet and couldn't drive that well. She ran after me yelling and waving he hands, "Come back here with my car, you turkey."

I heard once that to be demanded of gives you dignity. Deena demanded from herself and others that they did the best they could with themselves and their lives. The times I'd seen her seriously upset with others was when they were doing things to themselves, like taking drugs. She would be upset out of caring and not out of judgement.

We shared darker moments in our lives. I was living with her family the day her mother died. I didn't know what to say or to do so I just said, "Deena, I love you." We went driving in her car and Deena sang a hymn and I sang with her. Then Deena prayed and I just listened. That time in my life had been hard too. I'd gone away to school, San Luis Obispo, but I'd felt so out of it there that I didn't stay. I called Deena and she came to get me. I was scared and uncertain about my future. Staying with Deena and her family was a steady influence over me.

I decided to try school again and come to Humboldt. Deena teased me about it. She said, "You better be sure and stay there because that's too far for me to drive to pick you up." I remember the day I left I went to breakfast with Deena and some friends at Lido's, a restaurant where Deena worked. Then Deena took me to the bus depot. We hugged goodbye, Deena smiled, and I tried not to cry.

After I went to Humboldt State, Deena decided to transfer to Illinois State. Our last Christmas together we decided to formally adopt each other. I cut our fingers with a razor and I said some words that would make the adoption legitimate forever.

We shared a special time in our life. Our thoughts, hopes, beliefs, happy times and hard times. We shared our love and became sisters.

Love

One heart
Reaches
Another greets
In this way
Love can
Meet

Full of Grace

This church looks like the one in Ohio where I went with Grandma and Grandpa for mass. It's white, small with a big silver cross on top of its steeple. "Remember, Grandma? I remember standing on the church steps in Ohio with you and Grandpa said to the priest, 'This here's my favourite.'"

The kindly priest clasped my hand. "That makes you something really special." This holy water feels cool on my forehead. Her white hair covered with a black veil and her expression intent and serious, she kneels during mass on arthritic legs.

"Grandma, I came here to talk to you, to tell you goodbye. I wish I could have gone to the funeral." Where do I want to pray? By the Mother Mary statue or the Jesus statue? I'll pray by the Jesus statue with the thorns in his heart. It's quiet in here. There's a waiting air in here. I'm glad I'm the only one in this sanctuary.

"God, I know my grandma is with you now. Would you let her listen to me? Or if she can't, will you tell her what I say? I want to tell her goodbye.

Grandma, I'm sorry I didn't get to come and see you last summer... I wanted to; I just didn't have the money. I'm glad I could visit you three years ago in the summer and that we had all those talks. I'm glad I talked to you on Christmas Eve and told you I love you. I didn't know it was the last time I'd ever talk to you."

Heavy stones are pushing my heart together, tighter and

tighter. The red and blue colours of the stained-glass window are blending together inside my tears. In my red and blue tears, there are pictures of me with my grandma. I hear past exchanges. I hear my grandma. "It makes your grandpa nervous when you read so much. It's not good for you. It'll make your eyes weak."

I hear myself lying. "I have to read this, Grandma, it's for a book report." I'm sorry I lied about that. I think you knew I was lying.

I hear her again. "I need help washing my good dishes. They're all dusty."

I hear myself reluctantly responding. "All right, Grandma."

I see myself skipping home from school wearing long knee socks and a long skirt. I flop down on the couch in the front room holding my school books. My grandma is upset. She says, "You forgot to make your bed today. Those court people were here and wanted to see your room."

Now I hear Grandma and Grandpa telling me three summers ago, "They wanted to pay us. We told them we don't take no money for you are our kid. We don't take money to keep our own."

The candles are flickering around the feet of the statue of Jesus. They look beautiful to me, red and glowing. I want to say some more.

"Grandma, thank you for wanting me and especially for not wanting money for me. I'm glad you told me what you said to those people about the money.

It snowed here in Arcata on Thursday, the day you died. I was working at the Toddler Centre holding a baby when I looked out the window and saw rain turn into snow falling on the redwood trees. The snow reminded me of Ohio, of you. I didn't know, though, until Aunt Hilda told me that you'd died that day.

I hope you're happy, Grandma. I want you to know I'm doing the best I can with my life. I have the ring you and Aunt Mildred gave me. I wear it all the time… Someday I'll give it to my little girl when I have one and I'll tell her all about you. I love you, Grandma."

Oh, I forgot to bring matches. I want to light a candle. So just light one off another candle. Be careful, though. I tip the flame. I see the wick in the next candle catch.

A voice from my past echoes, "Your grandma lit candles and had a mass said for you, when you were in the hospital. You almost died."

"Grandma, I went through a tunnel that time when I was fourteen and I almost died but I didn't go all the way to the end. Something pulled me back. Maybe it was your prayers for me. Did you go through the same tunnel? Thank you for all your prayers for me; for loving me. I will miss you so much. This rosary's for you, Grandma. I know you're in heaven, not purgatory; but, I'll say it anyway 'cause I think it would make you happy."

This candle I lit is for you, too. I watch the candle's flame, steady and flickering while I feel a smooth bead on my rosary.

"Hail Mary full of grace
The lord is with thee
Blessed art thou
Among women
Blessed if the fruit of thy womb…"

Belonged

My grandma died today
What can I say?
About the Love she gave to me?
And how I can be strong and free
Because she cared
And we shared
A home
In my turning points of life
I stood alone
But strong
Because I belonged.

Other World

"Does Sharon know you're here?" Dee the secretary at EOP asked me.

"Yes, I think so," I said. I peeked around the corner into Sharon's office. She was talking to a student but I knew she'd seen me so I settled back to wait.

"I like this place," I thought. Everyone seemed very busy. Sometimes I talked to Dee or other people while I waited for Sharon but today, I didn't feel like talking. That was all right too.

The student walked out of Sharon's office. I went in. "Hi, Sharon," I said, glad to see her.

"Hi, Maya," she smiled at me, "I called you at the Children's Centre but you weren't there. Can I reschedule you? I'm supposed to go to the meeting for Native American College Motivation Day. They forgot to put it on the books."

I looked at the three falling beaded leaves hanging on Sharon's wall. I made the pattern and had done the beadwork on a loom. I gave them to Sharon five years ago as a Christmas present. I always feel happy when I look at the leaves.

I realized I hadn't answered Sharon yet. I looked at her. She frowned. What's wrong?" she asked me, concerned.

"I just had a bad day, Sharon. I wanted to be around you for a while."

"You wanted to be around someone who knows you and cares about you."

I nodded. "Yes"

"What happened?" she asked again, patient.

"My class is doing a drama about a hobo. You know, I explained, he doesn't have anywhere to live. I started to cry.

I remember things I don't want to remember." I stopped trying not to cry any more. "I think I'm too emotional now that I'm pregnant.

It's just a play to them. It hurts me too much," I said, feeling angry.

"Are you worried about your baby?" she asked.

"I don't want my baby to be on the streets," I answered.

"Your baby has a mother that loves it," Sharon said firmly. "That won't happen to your baby."

I gazed at Sharon's bookshelf, remembering.

I remembered fear and blood, enormous amounts of blood all over me. The cars whipped by me. I slid and slid on the asphalt. I stood up and ran and ran until I was off the freeway and onto a main street. I curled up on a bus bench to sleep. Not scared any more, I didn't feel anything. I noticed with curiosity that my hands didn't have any skin left.

"You know that time when I was a kid and I jumped out of a car?"

"Yes." She listened.

"Well, first they took me to the nearest hospital. It was private. They found out I didn't have medical insurance or parents and they didn't want me there. They said they couldn't treat me. I think, if I'd had parents with some insurance, they would have helped me. When I got to County Hospital, they put me on a red blanket."

"What does that mean?" asked Sharon.

"That means I had about five minutes to live without medical treatment."

"What was wrong?" she asked.

"I had internal bleeding and shock. The doctors kept asking where I lived. I told them, 'I don't live anywhere.'"

"That was hard, Maya, not fair. It shouldn't have happened to you," said Sharon.

"It wasn't just that one time, Sharon. It was my whole life."

"I know," she answered.

When I looked at Sharon's bookcase, another memory flashed by. The admitting nurse at East Los Angeles Juvenile Hall stuck a thermometer in my mouth while she took my blood pressure.

"Well," she smiled warmly at me, "I haven't seen you for a while. How old are you now?"

"Fourteen," I mumbled around the thermometer.

"You haven't gone off now and gotten yourself pregnant now, have you?" she asked in a half-serious and half-teasing voice. Her smile was warm.

"No," I smiled back at her, feeling somewhat proud of myself for not being pregnant.

She took the thermometer out of my mouth and frowned at it.

"Where you been sleeping, outside or inside?"

I shrugged.

She touched my hand. "I'm going to take you to the infirmary and have a doctor look at you. You'll have to stay there a while before going to receiving."

I nodded, a little surprised at this break in routine.

I strained to eavesdrop while she talked to the doctor in a lowered voice. "Police brought her in off the streets... high temp."

I could hear every other word. The whole memory flashed

by in less than a few seconds.

Sharon kept talking.

"I know it would be hard," she said. "It's hard for me to understand what it would feel like."

"I know," I thought. "You're related to everybody. How could you understand?" I thought, feeling amused with Sharon and how she was related to everybody. I smiled. I loved this lady that couldn't understand and was late for a meeting because she wanted to know what was wrong... because she cared.

"What are you thinking?" she asked, still serious.

"You should go to your meeting now, Sharon. I'll come to see you later. I'm OK now," I answered.

Outside again, I blinked at the redwood trees and blue sky a world away from the smoggy streets of LA. The memories faded away. "My baby will never know that world. She will belong, be secure, be loved. She will never know that other world," I promised myself. I promised my baby.

Ingram Content Group UK Ltd.
Milton Keynes UK
UKHW011931300623
424349UK00001B/43